Incredulità!

Utrolig!

NICHT WAHR!

Incroyable!

Ja nie wiezy!

HINDI KAPANIPANIWALA!

¡No es posible!

Mangel på tro!

Etä niuazmózhna!

Incrível!

Nie możliwie!

Would you believe!

NICHT WAHR!

Det är otroligt!

Incredità!

Utrolig!

Incrível!

Incroyable!

Ja nie wiezy!

HINDI KAPANIPANIWALA!

¡No es posible!

Mangel på tro!

Etä niuazmózhna!

Incrível!

Nie możliwie!

Would you believe!

NICHT WAHR!

Det är otroligt!

Would you Believe ?

By Isaac Asimov

Illustrated by Sam Sirdofsky Haffner

GROSSET & DUNLAP
Publishers • New York

1982 PRINTING

(The facts in this book are excerpted from *Isaac Asimov's Book of Facts*, published by Grosset & Dunlap, Inc.)

A tablet from ancient Assyria, about 2800 B.C., has been found that states: "Our earth is degenerate in these latter days. There are signs that the world is speedily coming to an end. Bribery and corruption are common." More than 2,000 years later, Socrates complained, "Children are now tyrants. . . . They no longer rise when elders enter the room. They contradict their parents, chatter before company, gobble up dainties at the table, cross their legs, and tyrannize over their teachers." And Plato wrote of his students: "What is happening to our young people? They disrespect their elders, they disobey their parents. They ignore the law. They riot in the streets inflamed with wild notions. Their morals are decaying. What is to become of them?"

According to Herodotus, the Babylonians had few doctors because they left illness to the wisdom of the public. A sick individual was placed in the city square, where passersby who had suffered from the same ailment, or had seen it treated, gave him advice on how to be cured. Pedestrians were forbidden to pass such an individual without inquiring about the complaint and "prescribing" for it if they could.

There were no garbage-disposal systems in the early towns of Mesopotamia. Rubbish accumulating in the streets was packed down by the comings and goings of men and animals. As the streets grew higher, the floors of houses had to be raised with additional layers of clay.

The Greek playwright Aeschylus, according to some sources, was killed by a tortoise. The animal, it is said, was dropped from the claws of an eagle flying overhead, which mistook Aeschylus' bald head for a rock.

A female pharaoh was unknown in Egypt before Hatshepsut, who began her reign in 1502 B.C. In order not to shock convention, she had herself portrayed in male costume, with a beard, and without breasts.

Queen Austrichildia, the wife of the Frankish King Guntram, was ill with dysentery in A.D. 580. She felt that her two physicians were not trying hard enough to cure her, so she extracted a promise from King Guntram to kill them, on her grave, if she died. The Queen did die, and the doctors were executed as she wished, in the presence of the other court doctors.

Louis IX, King of France (1226-70), was known as the saint-king. Louis wore a hair shirt, which helped, he said, to keep his mind on higher things. As a gesture of humility, he would kiss lepers and have poor people dine with him. So badly did some of the invited dregs of society smell that the soldiers of the guard (no flowers themselves) objected.

From the history of Babylonia comes the story of Enlil-Bani, King Erra-Immiti's gardener, who was chosen by him to be the "king for a day" as part of a New Year's celebration. According to custom, each mock king, after ruling for his day, was sacrificed to the gods. In Enlil-Bani's case, however, Erra-Immiti died during the celebration, and Enlil-Bani remained on the throne. He ruled well, for at least twenty-four years.

When they die, some fish spectacularly change colors. The dying mullet, for example, flashes patches of red, ocher, and green. In Roman days, the host at a posh banquet would have a still-living mullet brought in a vase to the table. When the water was removed from the vase, guests would watch the fish change colors as it gasped out its life. Pale in death, the mullet would be returned to the kitchen.

To make their parades more glamorous, the Sybarites taught their horses to dance rythmically to music. But when the Sybarite cavalry charged Croton, a city seventy miles to the south of Sybaris in Italy on the Gulf of Taranto, in 510 B.C., the men of Croton struck up a lively dance on their pipes and the Sybarite horses promptly fell to dancing. The charge was broken up, and the demoralized Sybarite army was slaughtered.

After becoming Emperor of Rome, Nero's dearest ambition was to sing in public, according to the Roman chronicler Suetonius. After taking lessons, he made his debut in Naples. An earth tremor shook the theater, causing some of the audience to depart while Nero continued singing. At a later performance elsewhere, he had the gates locked so no one could leave while he was on stage. Some women gave birth in the stands. Some men, tired out with listening and applauding, furtively leaped over the walls. Three clever citizens tricked the guards into letting them through an exit: one pretended to be dead and the other two carried him out.

Historians related the heart-warming story of Abdul Kassem Ismael (A.D. 938-95), the scholarly grand vizier of Persia, and his library of 117,000 volumes. On his many travels as a warrior and statesman, he never parted with his beloved books. They were carried about by 400 camels—trained to walk in a fixed order so that the books on their backs could be maintained in alphabetical order. The camel-driver librarians could put their hands instantly on any book their master asked for. Because of his friendly disposition, Abdul Kassem Ismael was nicknamed Saheb, "the pal."

Rules for parties during the reign of Catherine I of Russia (1725-27) declared that no gentleman was to get drunk before nine o'clock and that no lady was to get drunk at any hour. The Princess Elizabeth (Catherine's daughter) and the other young ladies of the court loved to dress up like young men, enabling them to circumvent the rules.

When Ivan the Terrible of Russia decided to marry, he directed all the nobles in his realm—those who refused faced execution—to send their marriageable daughters to Moscow. About 1,500 maidens were gathered in a huge building, where they slept twelve to a room. Ivan made his choice after inspecting the entire harem and presenting each with a gift, a kerchief embroidered with gold and gems. After the deaths of his first and second wives, he selected a third in the same manner. She became mortally ill when she learned of the czar's decision to choose her and died in 1569 before the marriage was consummated.

Admiral Sir Cloudesley Shovel, commander-in-chief of the British fleet, was murdered in 1707 by an old woman as he struggled ashore after the loss of his ship on the rocks of the Scilly Islands. She killed him in the belief, current at the time among coastal inhabitants, that a body washed up was a derelict, thus giving her legal possession of the emerald ring on the admiral's finger.

On July 4, 1776, George III of England wrote in his diary, "Nothing of importance happened today." He had no way of knowing what had occurred that day in Philadelphia, Pennsylvania.

Czar Peter III of Russia ruled six months, then was murdered in June 1762 at the age of thirty-four through the conspiracy of his wife, Catherine. He was not crowned until thirty-five years after his death, when his coffin was opened expressly for that purpose.

During her tour of the Russian provinces in 1787, Catherine the Great, seeing joyful people and prosperous villages, believed she had succeeded in making her subjects happy. She did not realize it was all a sham concocted by her prime minister, the one-eyed Gregory Potemkin, who had "Potemkin villages" prepared along the royal route. He had ordered the people to clean the streets, paint the fronts of their houses, wear their best clothes, and smile. The Empress never noticed the misery and squalor behind the facade.

The American paleontologist, Edward Cope (1840-97), was a Quaker and consequently refused to carry a gun during his U.S. Western expeditions, despite the very real danger from Indians. He once flabbergasted hostile Indians surrounding him by removing his false teeth and putting them back, over and over. The Indians let him go.

A chief of the Omaha Indian tribe, Blackbird, was buried sitting on his favorite horse.

In 1909, Annette Kellerman, the Australian swimming star, appeared on a Boston beach wearing a figure-fitting jersey bathing suit with sleeves shortened almost to her shoulders and trousers ending two inches above her knees. She was arrested for indecent exposure.

Town laws in the U.S. Midwest in the 1880s were passed prohibiting the sale of ice-cream sodas on Sunday. In Illinois, ingenious soda fountain owners got around the law by omitting the carbonated water and serving just the scoop of ice cream and the syrup. They called this a "Sunday soda." Later that name was shortened to "Sunday," and then it became "sundae."

Dr. James Barry, a woman posing as a man, became a general in the army of Queen Victoria. Barry entered the medical corps, served forty years as a surgeon, and rose to the rank of inspector-general of hospitals. Only after Barry's death in 1865 was "his" true sex discovered.

The future U.S. General Douglas MacArthur was dressed in skirts by his mother until he was eight years old.

For the first six years of his life, the greatest lyric poet of modern Germany, Rainer Maria Rilke (1875-1926), was treated by his mother like a girl; he was called "Sophie" and kept in girl's dresses. In his mother's fancy, he was replacing a sister who had died before Rainer was born.

King Alfonso of Spain, who reigned from 1886 to 1931, was so tone-deaf that he had one man in his employ known as the Anthem Man. This man's sole duty was to tell the king to stand up whenever the Spanish national anthem was played, because the monarch couldn't recognize it.

Until 1826, white people in the United States were sold as indentured servants who would be freed after a certain period of time. Andrew Johnson, who became president in 1865, was a runaway indentured servant; advertisements appeared in newspapers in an attempt to get him back.

No matter where she went—and she went as far afield as the Crimea in 1854 —the "Lady of the Lamp," the English hospital administrator and reformer Florence Nightingale, carried a pet owl in a pocket.

In fourteenth-century France, Philip the Fair forbade dukes, counts, barons, and their wives to own more than four garments; unmarried women could own only one dress, unless they were heiresses who had inherited castles. His edicts did not mention shoes, however, and they became a symbol of elegance. Named after its inventor, the *poulaine* was a shoe whose tip was as long as two feet for princes and noblemen, one foot for rich people of lower degree, and only half a foot for common people. Such extravagances proved a hazard among the French Crusaders at the battle of Nicopolis (1396) when they had to cut off the tips of their shoes in order to be able to run away.

When Elizabeth I of Russia died in 1762, 15,000 dresses were found in her closets. She used to change what she was wearing two and even three times an evening.

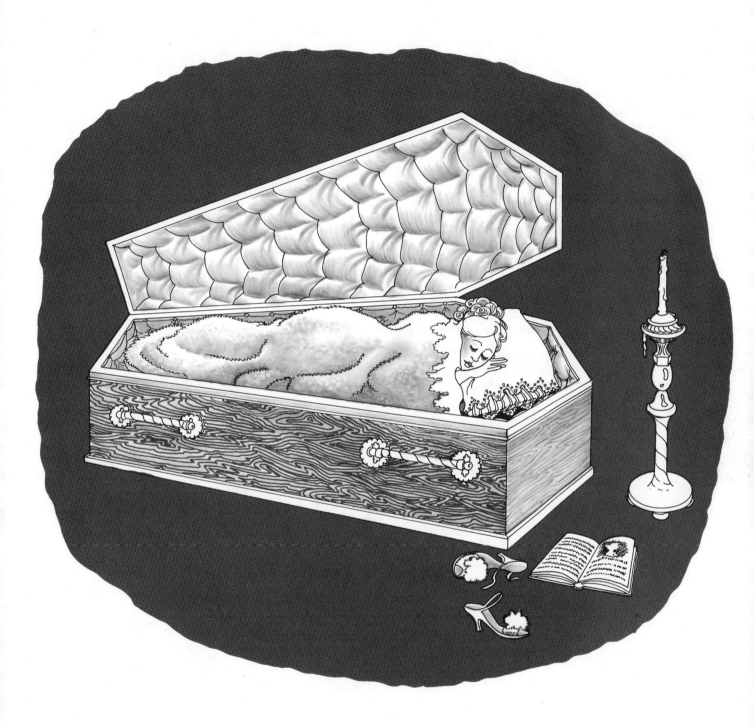

The great French actress Sarah Bernhardt was obsessed with death. As a teen-
ager, she made frequent visits to the Paris morgue to look at corpses of der-
elicts dragged up from the Seine, and she begged her mother to buy her a
pretty rosewood coffin with a white satin lining. The coffin became part of the
Bernhardt legend. Occasionally, she slept in it, and eventually she was buried
in it when she died at seventy-nine.

President Ulysses S. Grant's wife was cross-eyed and wanted to correct the problem. Grant refused to let her have the operation because he liked her that way.

Because of his spindly arms and legs, the satirist Alexander Pope was described as a "crazy little carcass" of a man. To keep his miniature body erect, he wore stiff canvas. To swell his pin-sized legs to something approaching normal, he wore three pairs of stockings.

The father of Frederick the Great had a famous private guard company—the Potsdam Grenadiers. He would bribe, buy, or even kidnap tall men, close to seven feet in height, to get them for the Grenadiers. He also made the giant men marry giant women so he could "raise" his own giants.

Ladies in Europe took to wearing lightning rods on their hats and trailing a ground wire—a fad that began after Benjamin Franklin published instructions on how to make them, in his almanac, *Poor Richard Improved,* in 1753.

The Padaung people of Burma believe that a long neck is beautiful. When a woman is young, she has a brass ring fastened around her neck. Over the years, rings are added until the neck becomes elongated and beauty is achieved. She also wears brass rings around her legs, and daily carries around about twenty pounds of brass.

So they would have a fashionably flat skull, infants in the Chinook Indian tribe were strapped between boards from head to toe, until they were about a year old.

President William Howard Taft weighed 350 pounds. He once got stuck in a bathtub in the White House and someone had to be called to pull him out. He then had a special tub made. It was so big that, when it was delivered, four White House workmen climbed into it and had their picture taken.

When Taft was president of the Philippine Commission in 1900, Secretary of War Elihu Root cabled him to ask how he was—Root had heard that Taft was ill. Taft reassured Root by cabling that he was much better and that he had, in fact, just returned from a twenty-five-mile ride on horseback. Elihu Root cabled back: "How is the horse?"

Pepin the Short, King of the Franks (A.D. 751-768), was short indeed—all of four feet, six inches. Yet he carried a six-foot-long sword and was a mighty warrior —and the father of Charlemagne.

A dwarf eighteen inches high served as a captain of cavalry in the British army. He was Jeffery Hudson, and he lived from 1619 to 1682. He made his first recorded appearance when he was served inside a pie at the table of the Duke of Buckingham. Later, when he was about thirty years old, he grew to more than twice his earlier adult height—to three feet, nine inches.

He
—lost his job in 1832.
—was defeated for the legislature in 1832.
—failed in business in 1833.
—suffered a nervous breakdown in 1836.
—was defeated for speaker of the Illinois state legislature in 1838.
—was defeated for nomination for Congress in 1843.
—lost renomination to Congress in 1848.
—was rejected for land office in 1849.
—was defeated for the Senate in 1854.
—was defeated for nomination for vice-president in 1856.
—was defeated for the Senate in 1858.
—became the sixteenth president of the U.S. in 1861.

O.J. Simpson had a severe case of rickets and wore leg braces when he was a child. Simpson went on to set ground-gaining records in the National Football League.

Glenn Cunningham was badly burned when he was eight years old and was told he would never walk again; in fact, it took him more than two years simply to straighten out his right leg. Cunningham went on to become one of the greatest all-time mile runners, holder at one time of five world track records.

Hans Christian Andersen's fairy tales were greeted by bad reviews: ". . . quite unsuitable for children . . . positively harmful for the mind. . . ."

Thomas Alva Edison was one of a fair number of geniuses who did poorly in school. (Einstein, Newton, and Pasteur were three others.) In fact, Edison's mother, a schoolteacher, was so offended with the bad reports young Tom was getting at school that she took him out of school altogether and taught him herself.

He didn't care much about his studies, and indeed never finished high school. Because he spent more time reading and gossiping with friends than sticking to his job, he was not continued as the community postmaster. "I will be damned," he said after losing the job, "if I propose to be at the beck and call

of every itinerant scoundrel who has two cents to invest in a postage stamp."
In 1949, he was awarded the Nobel Prize for literature—his name was William
Faulkner.

Émile Zola received a zero in French literature and failed German and rhetoric
at the Lycée St. Louis.

Beethoven as a child made such a poor impression on his music teachers that
he was pronounced hopeless as a composer. Even Haydn, who taught him
harmony for a time, did not recognize Beethoven's potential genius.

Cézanne was turned down by the École des Beaux-Arts when he applied for
entrance.

David ———— (his last name has never been publicly revealed) has lived all of his life in a sterile environment. He suffers from the rare disease known as severe combined immune deficiency, and his body is unable to fight off even the most common germs. (By living in a germfree life-support system, which is enclosed in a see-through plastic bubble, he has never experienced a sick day, except for his disease, for which doctors say there is still no treatment.) On his seventh birthday, in 1978, he wasn't able to blow out the candles on his cake—they weren't allowed in the bubble, so he was only able to see them. About a hundred people are known to have been born with the blood disorder, and David is the oldest of five survivors. David lives with his family in Houston, and walks out of doors wearing an astronaut's suit with a plastic-bubble helmet.

The Winchester House, near San Jose, California, is perhaps the most bizarre house ever built. Mrs. Sara Winchester was convinced that if she stopped adding rooms to her house, she would die. So every day for thirty-eight years construction went on. The house contains 2,000 doors and 10,000 windows, many of which open onto blank walls, and stairways that lead nowhere. The eight-story house has forty-eight fireplaces and miles of secret passages and hallways. When Mrs. Winchester died, in 1922, at the age of eighty-five, her mansion contained 160 rooms and covered over six acres of ground.

In 1911, a suburban tailor named Teichelt, who had invented a batwing cape that he believed would enable him to fly, applied for permission to fly from the Eiffel Tower. The proprietors of the tower reluctantly gave permission, provided that Teichelt obtain police authorization and that he sign a waiver absolving the tower proprietors. Incredibly, the police gave permission. At eight o'clock, on a cold December morning, Teichelt—accompanied by a handful of well-wishers and press photographers—climbed to the level of the first platform, stepped over the edge, and plunged to his death.

Every four or five years, the Malagasy of the Indian Ocean island of Madagascar, off southeast Africa, retrieve their dead from tombs that are half above ground and half below, expose them to the sunlight, toss them and catch them, and then wrap them in new silk for reinternment. The ritual is called *famadihana,* and it is a time of much celebration, with singing and dancing.

Emperor Caligula made his favorite horse, Incitatus, a consul and coregent of Rome. The horse, which was accorded honor at every turn, had an ivory manger and a golden drinking goblet for wine.

The Egyptians trained baboons to wait on tables.

One of the most famous dogs who ever lived was a homeless Skye terrier named Bobby. As a puppy, he attached himself to an elderly Scottish shepherd named Auld Jock. Jock died in 1858, and for the next fourteen years Bobby guarded his master's grave day and night. He would leave it briefly each day, only to go to the same restaurant where his master used to go. He'd be given food and would eat it near the grave. The citizens of Edinburgh erected a shelter to shield Bobby from the cold winters, and when he died in 1872, he was buried beside Auld Jock.

The Pilgrims did not build log cabins, nor did they wear black hats with a conical crown and a hatband with a silver buckle.

Though popularly thought to have been an Egyptian, Cleopatra was a Macedonian, the daughter of Ptolemy XI. She married two of her brothers and was the mistress of both Julius Caesar and Mark Antony.

Samuel F.B. Morse did not really invent the telegraph. He managed to get all the necessary information for the invention from the American physicist Joseph Henry, and later denied that Henry had helped him. (Henry easily proved the contrary in a court trial.)

James Watt did not invent the steam engine; Thomas Newcomen did, in 1712. Watt devised a modified engine that was much more efficient and that could be used to turn wheels. This modified steam engine was so useful that the earlier Newcomen engine was soon forgotten.

Robert Fulton did not invent the steamship. Seventeen years before Fulton's first ship sailed up the Hudson River, John Fitch maintained a regular steamship schedule on the Delaware River between Philadelphia and Trenton.

Betsy Ross did not design the American flag, Francis Hopkinson of New Jersey did. Elizabeth Griscom Ross—"Betsy"—was merely the seamstress. The family legend that made Betsy Ross famous was first told thirty years after her death. A grandson claimed that she had been visited in June 1776 by a secret committee, which included George Washington, that asked her to design and sew the flag for the new nation. There is no evidence to confirm the story.

The president of Memorial Sloan-Kettering Cancer Center in New York, which specializes in cancer treatment, has observed that "ants are so much like human beings as to be an embarrassment." Writes Dr. Lewis Thomas: "[Ants] farm fungi, raise aphids as livestock, launch armies into wars, use chemical sprays to alarm and confuse enemies, and capture slaves. The families of weaver ants engage in child labor, holding their larvae like shuttles to spin out the thread that sews the leaves together for their fungus gardens. They exchange information ceaselessly. They do everything but watch television."

The male praying mantis often loses his head—literally—after courting the female. She is known to decapitate the earnest suitor and often completely devours him.

When a queen bee lays the fertilized eggs that will develop into new queens, only one of the newly laid queens actually survives. The first new queen that emerges from her cell destroys all other queens in their cells and, thereafter, reigns alone.

The female pigeon cannot lay eggs if she is alone. In order for her ovaries to function, she must be able to see another pigeon. If no other pigeon is available, her own reflection in a mirror will suffice.

A newborn turkey chick has to be taught to eat, or it will starve. Breeders spread feed underfoot, hoping the little ones will peck at it and get the idea. Turkeys tend to look up with their mouths open during rainstorms. Lots of them drown as a result.

Birds played a role in aerial warfare during World War I. Because of their acute hearing, parrots were kept on the Eiffel Tower to warn of approaching aircraft long before the planes were heard or seen by human spotters.

Human beings are not the only animals that sometimes abuse their children. The Yerkes Regional Primate Research Center in Atlanta, Georgia, concludes from studies of mother-infant relationships among the seventeen lowland gorillas at the center that abuse by gorilla mothers seems to be the norm when the animals are caged alone with their babies. By contrast, mothers in groups displayed loving, nurturing behavior toward their infants.

The honey ant of the desert has an unusual method of providing food in times of scarcity. Certain members of the colony are stuffed with liquid food or water until the rear portions of their bodies are enlarged to the size of a pea. When a famine occurs, these ants disgorge their supplies to feed the others.

A mosquito has forty-seven teeth.

Cockroaches have quite a capacity for survival. If the head of one is removed carefully, so as to prevent it from bleeding to death, the cockroach can survive for several weeks. When it dies, it is from starvation.

Three months after they have been laid, crocodile eggs are ready to be hatched. But the baby crocodiles cannot dig away the sand above them. They peep while still inside their shells, and their mother, who has been guarding them, hears their calls and digs them free.

Toads and frogs use their eyes to eat with. In swallowing, they close their eyelids, press down with their extremely tough eyeballs, and lower the roof of their mouth against their tongue, forcing the food down and into their stomach.

Black sea bass, when young, are preponderantly female. At the age of five years or so, many switch sex and become functional males.

The female anglerfish is six times larger than her mate. The male anchors himself to the top of her head and stays there for the rest of his life. They literally become one. Their digestive and circulatory systems are merged. Except for two very large generative organs and a few fins, nothing remains of the male.

The oyster is usually ambisexual. It begins life as a male, then becomes a female, then changes back to being a male, then back to being a female; it may go back and forth many times.

It is the female lion who does more than ninety percent of the hunting, while the male is afraid to risk his life or simply prefers to rest.

"One of the most beautiful sights is a urine dump at sunset, because as the stuff comes out [in space], and as it hits the exit nozzle, it instantly flashes into ten million little ice crystals, which go out almost in a hemisphere, because, you know, you're exiting into essentially a perfect vacuum, and so the stuff goes in every direction, and radially out from the spacecraft at relatively high velocity. It's surprising, it's an incredible stream . . . a spray of sparklers almost. It's really a spectacular sight."

—Russell Schweickart, Apollo astronaut

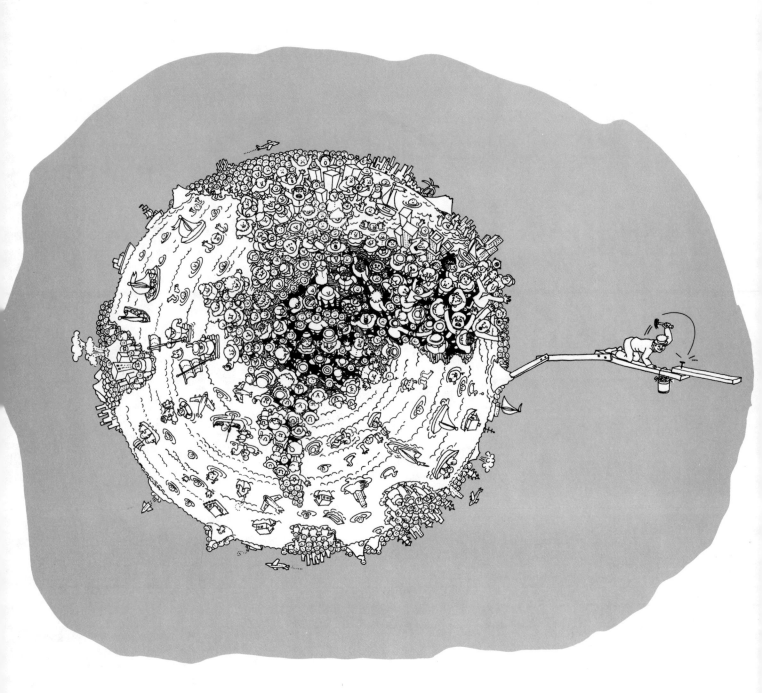

If the population of the Earth were to continue to increase at the present rate indefinitely, by A.D. 3530 the total mass of human flesh and blood would equal the mass of the Earth. By A.D. 6826, the total mass of human flesh and blood would equal the mass of the known universe.

Mangel på tro!

Etä nivazmózhna!

Incrível!

Nie możliwie!

Would you believe!

NICHT WAHR!

Det är otroligt!

Incredulità!

Utrolig!

Nie możliwie!

Ja nie wiezy!

Incroyable!

¡No es posible!

HINDI KAPANIPANIWALA!

Etä nivazmózhna!

Mangel på tro!

Nie możliwie!

Incrível!

NICHT WAHR!

Would you believe!

Det är otroligt!

Incredulità!

Utrolig!

¡No es posible!

Ja nie wiezy!

Incroyable!

HINDI KAPANIPANIWALA!

¡No es posible!